THE ADVENTURES OF
PINOCCHIO™

THE ADVENTURES OF PINOCCHIO™

A novelization by J.J. Gardner
Based on the screenplay by
Sherry Mills & Steve Barron and Barry Berman

SCHOLASTIC INC.
New York Toronto London Auckland Sydney

ISBN 0-590-92264-5

12 11 10 9 8 7 6 5 4 3 2 1   6 7 8 9/9 0 1/0

Printed in the U.S.A.   40

First Scholastic printing, August 1996

THE ADVENTURES OF

PINOCCHIO™

PART ONE:
THE PUPPET MAKER

1.
The Forest

In a pine forest outside his little village in Italy, Geppetto the puppet maker was collecting wood.

To old Geppetto, the pine forest was a magical place. Each morning, just before dawn, he woke up early and went there. At that time of day there were still shiny droplets of dew dripping from the leaves of the great pine trees. The deep scent of pine drifted on the gentle morning breezes.

The forest never disappointed the old puppet maker. There were always plenty of small logs and branches for him to collect. Some of the better ones he would use to carve parts for his puppets. Others he would sell as firewood in the village square. The rest he would burn in his own fireplace to keep his workshop warm.

One day, when he had collected enough wood, Geppetto began to wheel his pushcart away. He stopped when he saw a young couple sitting beneath a tree. The two were obviously very much

3

in love, and the young man was carving their initials into a fallen log.

When the young couple saw Geppetto, they became startled and got up to leave.

"Hold on, you two!" Geppetto called in a stern voice. "Come back here!"

"Yes, *signore*?" the boy asked timidly.

"I'm trying to get to the west side of the forest," replied Geppetto. "But some nincompoop took down the sign at the pond."

"West is that way," said the boy, pointing.

"That's north!" Geppetto exclaimed with a laugh. "West is the other way. I know this forest like the back of my hand."

"Anything you say, *signore*," said the boy, bewildered. Then he and his young lady headed away as fast as they could.

Geppetto laughed again. "Young folks today don't know anything," he muttered to himself.

But when Geppetto tried to wheel his pushcart away, it wouldn't move. He tried again, but still it would not budge. Finally, he looked down and saw that the same log the boy had carved his initials into had become wedged against one of the wheels of the pushcart. Geppetto noticed that the log was covered with many initials chiseled into it by countless other couples over time. Geppetto smiled warmly, remembering that he too had once carved initials into a tree in this very same forest.

But then his smile faded. It had been a long

time since he was a young man. Sadly, the years that followed had brought him no lasting love, no marriage, no children. He suddenly felt very lonesome and alone in the great pine forest.

He picked up the old log and threw it into his pushcart with the other scraps. It would make good firewood, he thought.

Then he wheeled his pushcart back toward the village.

2.
The Workshop

Upon returning to the village square, Geppetto sold most of the wood he had collected. By the time he got to his workshop, the only piece remaining was the old log.

Geppetto was glad to be home. "Yoo-hoo, everybody. I'm home!" he announced cheerily as he entered his house.

But the old puppet maker was greeted with the same dead silence he had become so used to over the years. For nobody lived with Geppetto. Nobody *real*, that is. Instead, Geppetto's walls were occupied with shelves and shelves of beautiful puppets and marionettes, all of which he had hand-crafted himself.

"Fine," Geppetto said grumpily to a row of puppet boys. "Don't say hello." And with that he placed his log and a basket of groceries on a worktable.

There were two marionettes on the worktable.

They were tangled together in such a way that it looked as if they had just had a brawl.

"Are you two arguing again?" Geppetto asked the marionettes as he untangled them. "What's the problem this time?"

"He said I had a funny nose," said Geppetto in a squeaky voice. He was pretending that one of the puppets was answering him.

"I said you had funny *toes*," Geppetto made the second puppet reply.

"What's the difference?" Geppetto said to the puppets in a fatherly voice. "I'm tired of hearing you two fight. I think you should both apologize. Hey! Stop that!"

With a tug of their strings, Geppetto had made it appear as if the two puppets were wrestling each other. Geppetto smiled warmly. He maneuvered the two puppets apart as if they were a couple of unruly brothers.

To him they *were* brothers. They were the sons he never had.

"All right," said Geppetto. "You know what happens to boys who fight. They go to bed without being sandpapered."

With that, Geppetto chuckled softly and returned the puppets to their places on the wall. For a long moment, he looked at them with affection. He wished, as he often did, that they could be real human boys, not puppets. Then, with a heavy sigh, he carried his log to the fireplace and tossed it in.

"Burn," he ordered the log. Then he stoked the ashes around it with a poker. Suddenly a burst of flames ignited around the aged bark of the log. The fire crackled and raged, and without warning the old log jumped from the fireplace and landed right at Geppetto's feet.

"This log has a will of its own," said Geppetto as he leaned down and examined it. For the first time he noticed that a long branch stuck out at one end of the log. In the shadows created by the bright fire, the branch looked to Geppetto like a very long nose.

But that wasn't all. All of a sudden, the log took on a whole new set of features in Geppetto's eyes. The branch was a nose. The knotholes just above it were eyes. A jagged cranny that ran across the trunk could almost be a mouth. There was even a heart-shaped carving farther down, no doubt chiseled by some romantic young couple in years gone by. Some embers, still red hot from the fireplace, were caught in the grooves of the heart. The heart seemed to glow and pulsate as if it were alive.

Geppetto noticed something that made his own heart skip a beat. Two initials were carved inside the heart: L & G. He recognized the carving instantly. It was his own, made when he was a young man in love. But in those days he had carved his initials into a tall, standing tree, green with life. This dead log was all that remained of that tree and his youth.

"I guess we've all been young and foolish at one time," he muttered thoughtfully. Then he turned to his other puppets and said, "Anyone who wants another brother, say so now."

Geppetto didn't wait for an answer. Instead, he laid the log on his worktable and began carving into it with his chisel.

"I must give you the most perfect nose," he said to the log as he began to work.

Geppetto worked for the rest of the afternoon and on through the night.

3.
The New Puppet

It was early dawn by the time Geppetto put the last touch of paint on his newly made puppet boy. When he was finished, he stood back and admired his work. The puppet's eyes were wide and bright, as if they were seeing the world for the first time. Its hair was a golden brown, as if untouched by age. And its mouth was fixed with a cheerful smile, as if it had never known sadness.

But something was wrong with its nose. "Noses were never my strong point," Geppetto muttered to himself as he leaned in and made an adjustment on the puppet's nose. "There. That's better. A world of wisdom is told in a nose."

Geppetto smiled with pride. The puppet was among the finest he had ever made. There was something about it that seemed extra special. He wasn't sure why, but this puppet seemed more human-looking than any of the others.

If it were a real boy, Geppetto thought, what a fine-looking son this puppet would make.

Geppetto attached a cross-tree with marionette strings to the puppet and stood it up. "Nice posture, son," he said with affection. "Would you like your papa to show you how to walk?"

Geppetto tugged at the cross-tree and made the puppet nod yes. "Very nice," said Geppetto with a smile. "Such a smart little boy you are."

He turned to his other puppets. He imagined them all waiting eagerly to meet their new brother. "Excuse me," he said to his new puppet. "Coming through." And with that he walked the puppet over to the others, just as a real father might take a son to his first day of school.

"Say hello to your brothers and sisters," Geppetto told the new puppet. "They'll keep you company while I'm out working. Now what shall we name you, dear child? You're made of pine, that's a start. You've got such big eyes. *Occhi magnificchi* . . . we'll call you Pinocchio! Yes!"

Geppetto was tired after spending the night creating his new puppet boy. What he needed now, he decided, was a hot bath, a meal, and some sleep. He set Pinocchio on his worktable, then took a kettle from the stove and filled his bathtub with hot water.

As Geppetto sank into the soothing water of the bathtub, he closed his eyes and sighed. Having a new puppet in the family made him feel less lonely. True, Pinocchio was only a boy made of wood and paint, but somehow Geppetto felt as if the new puppet needed him. It was the way he felt about all his creations. They were all his children.

And they were so well-behaved. "Much better to have puppets than noisy little boys running around," he muttered to himself. He was immensely satisfied.

PART TWO:
THE PUPPET BOY

4.
Coming to Life

The puppet boy opened his eyes and saw the world for the very first time.

The first thing he saw was a bright light coming through a large square opening several feet away. It was the morning sun shining through a window. It felt good and warm on his face.

Everything else around him was dark and new and very strange. All around him were all sorts of objects that were nothing less than a mystery to him. Some were round, some square. Some were large and some were small. Some were very high and some were very low. From the high spot where he was sitting, the world seemed like a cluttered place.

But where *was* he sitting, he wondered? He didn't know. Nor did he know how he came to be there, wherever *there* might be. In fact, it occurred to him that he didn't even know his own name or what he looked like.

The puppet boy felt very alone.

He decided that if he was going to find out anything, like where he was or even who he was, he must move. But when he lifted his arm, something kept it from moving very far. He tried again, but still he could move his arm only an inch here or an inch there. He looked down and saw that not only his arms, but his legs as well, were attached to a strange wooden cross by some long thin strings. With determination, he gave his arm a forceful tug. One of the strings snapped, and suddenly his arm was free.

The puppet boy felt excited. Now nothing could stop him from breaking free of the other strange strings that held his tiny body. He took a deep breath and tugged with all his strength.

All at once he broke free of the strings with such force that he went tumbling forward and over the edge of the high place where he was sitting.

KA-WOOSH! He landed faceup in a pile of sawdust on the floor. For a moment he just lay there while he tried to figure out his next move.

It was then that he heard a strange sound. He had never heard a sound like that before (in fact, he had never heard *any* sounds before). There was something pleasing about it. It almost made him feel like dancing.

The puppet boy stood straight up. He twisted his head completely around (it had been twisted backward during the fall). Then he turned in the direction of the sound, which was coming from behind a curtain a few feet away.

" 'Scuse me," said the puppet boy out loud. "Coming through!"

And with that he took a wobbly first step, then another and another. Before he knew it, he had reached the curtains.

The puppet boy peeked through the curtain. A figure, certainly twice his size if not more, was sitting in a huge metal bowl that was filled with steamy water. The puppet boy realized that, in many ways, the figure looked a lot like him. It had two arms and two legs and a round head at the top.

The figure reached across for a small, white, sudsy bar that was floating on the water. Because of a cloth that covered his face, the figure was unable to see the bar. Each time he reached for it, he missed.

The puppet boy decided to help and handed the figure the bar.

"Thank you," said the figure. "Now may I have the scrub brush — "

The figure stopped, surprised that there was another person in the room with him. He cautiously lifted the wet washcloth from his face and peeked out.

"Scubbwush," the puppet boy offered politely.

17

5.
A Very
Curious Puppet

The puppet boy gleefully leaped into the wash-tub, splashing water all about as he did so.

"It's happened," said Geppetto, bounding out of the tub. "I've finally lost my mind."

He quickly put on his bathrobe and eyeglasses and stared at the puppet boy, his creation come to life. The puppet was sitting on top of the water, floating like a toy duck.

"This is impossible," said Geppetto, bewildered. He waved his hands around the puppet checking for strings, but there were none. "You can't be real!"

"Real," the puppet boy said proudly.

"But you're a puppet!" exclaimed Geppetto.

"Pup . . . puppe . . . Papa!" the puppet tried repeating.

"Papa?" said Geppetto. "I'm not your papa!" Then Geppetto thought: *But in a way, it's true. I created you. I am a kind of papa.* He was pleased by the thought.

Just then the puppet boy caught sight of a pigeon that had come to rest on a windowsill.

" 'Scuse me!" he shouted with excitement. "Coming through!"

And with that he leaped out of the bathtub and reached for the bird just as it flew away.

"Wait!" Geppetto shouted. "Stop!"

But it was too late. Pinocchio had climbed through the window and was gone.

Geppetto raced outside and searched for Pinocchio. The puppet boy was clinging to the outside of the building, climbing the gutter spout toward the roof.

"Come down here this instant, young man!" demanded Geppetto. "I'm not going to chase after you!"

By now some of the people in the street had gathered around to see what all the commotion was about. They were obviously surprised to see Geppetto shouting up at a little boy who was made all of wood.

Pinocchio teetered along the roof tiles, all the while keeping careful sight of the pigeon as it bobbed away from him. For a moment, he lost his footing and nearly slid off the building.

"Hang on!" shouted Geppetto. "I'll save you! Don't panic!"

But Pinocchio wasn't scared. Instead, he grabbed hold of the side of the roof and pulled himself back up. He now had the pigeon cornered.

Gleefully, he reached out to grab the bird, but the pigeon flapped its wings and soared into the sky.

Pinocchio wanted to fly, too. So he imitated the pigeon and began to flap his thin wooden arms as if they were wings. Then he leaped off the roof. But instead of soaring into the sky, Pinocchio plummeted downward into a courtyard. Fortunately for him, his fall was broken by a row of laundry that had been hung out to dry.

Geppetto had seen the whole thing and feared the worst. But when he arrived at the courtyard, he saw that, except for a bolt that had slipped out of one of his legs, Pinocchio was unharmed. And the only thing out of place was the underpants Pinocchio was now wearing for a hat.

"All right, now listen, Pinocchio," Geppetto said sternly as he pulled the underwear off the puppet's head.

" 'Pinocchio,' " repeated the puppet. It was the first time he had ever heard his name.

"Right. Now, listen — " said Geppetto. He was trying his best to sound like a scolding father.

"Papa!" Pinocchio said, pointing to Geppetto.

"No! I mean, well, yes, in a manner of speaking. But don't call me Papa."

"Pa pa pa pa pa pa pa pa Papa," said Pinocchio.

"You're a puppet, Pinocchio," insisted Geppetto. "You're not a real boy."

Pinocchio wasn't sure what Geppetto meant by that. "Real boy?" he asked.

"No," replied Geppetto as he screwed the loose bolt back into Pinocchio's leg. "And be glad of it. If you were a real boy, you'd need a doctor instead of a puppet maker. Now sit still."

"Another new puppet, Geppetto?" came a familiar voice from behind.

Geppetto turned around. It was Leona, his widowed sister-in-law. Geppetto was secretly in love with her, but he didn't show it.

"He still needs a little work," explained Geppetto, as he made sure Pinocchio's leg joint was fastened tight.

"So do you," said Leona. "Look at you. Were you up all night again?"

"I slept a little."

"You *were* up all night," Leona said. Then she pulled some tiny clothes from the clothesline and handed them to Geppetto. "Here. I made these to sell to Lorenzini and his traveling puppet show, but I think your puppet needs them more."

"Thank you," Geppetto said, taking the clothes.

"You're welcome. And I'll bet there's sawdust all over your house. I'll come by and sweep it up."

"Leona, I'm not a child," Geppetto said stubbornly.

"So does the little one have a name?" Leona asked.

"Real boy!" said Pinocchio, announcing himself proudly.

"His name is Pinocchio," Geppetto corrected.

21

Leona extended her hand to the puppet. "Enchanted. My name is Leona."

Then, much to her surprise, Pinocchio extended his hand right back.

"You have even given him your heart," Leona said to Geppetto. She noticed the heart with "L & G" carved into Pinocchio's chest.

"*Our* heart," Geppetto mumbled, almost loud enough for Leona to hear.

"What did you say?" asked Leona.

"Nothing," said Geppetto. "Let's go, Pinocchio."

Geppetto took Pinocchio by the hand and walked off without so much as saying good-bye to Leona. As he led his puppet boy home, he found himself remembering that day long ago when he and Leona were both young. It was their initials he had once carved into that tree. In those days he had been too shy to ask her to marry him, so she married his brother instead. Years later, after his brother passed away, Geppetto found that he was still in love with her.

But even as an old man, he was still too shy to tell her.

6.
The Very
Mysterious Couple

Pinocchio followed Geppetto as they walked through the village square, but it wasn't long before he realized that he wasn't alone. Behind him, a trail of townspeople had gathered. They all seemed to be staring at him.

Pinocchio was fascinated by the townspeople. There were tall people and short people, fat people and thin people, old people and young people. But of all the people, he was most fascinated by a little boy who had stopped right in front of him. In almost every way, the boy looked just like Pinocchio. The only difference was that he wasn't made of wood.

"Are you a real boy?" Pinocchio asked.

"Yes," replied the boy. "Are you?"

"Yes," answered Pinocchio proudly.

The boy had a small red ball, which he threw at Pinocchio. The ball ricocheted off Pinocchio's head and bounced down a row of cobblestone steps. Pinocchio broke away from Geppetto and

23

chased after the ball just as fast as his wooden legs would take him. *Clip-clop.*

"Hellooooooo," he heard a voice say as he reached the bottom of the stairs. A mysterious-looking woman was standing there holding the red ball in her hand. Beside her was a short, fat, but equally mysterious-looking little man.

"What an intriguing-looking item you are," the woman said to Pinocchio. "May I?"

And with that the woman knocked three times on Pinocchio's wooden head. It sounded almost as if she were knocking on somebody's front door.

"Empty," said the woman.

"Must be those new invisible strings," said the little man, when he noticed that the puppet boy had no strings.

Pinocchio reached for the red ball in the woman's hand, but she quickly snatched it away.

"Ooh," she said. "Look how smoothly his arms move."

Just then Pinocchio saw Geppetto come running down the stairs.

"Felinet, excuse me," he said to the woman as he squeezed past her. Pinocchio could see that Geppetto did not like the mysterious woman and the little man. "And Volpe, haven't you got something better to do? Like robbing a pushcart?"

"We've already done that," said Volpe.

"Come, Pinocchio," said Geppetto, taking Pinocchio by the hand.

"But, Geppetto, darling," said Felinet. "We were just playing with him."

"He'll play with his own sort, thank you," said Geppetto sharply.

"And what would that sort be?" asked Felinet.

Without answering her, Geppetto scooped up Pinocchio in his arms. Then he carried his puppet boy all the way back up the cobblestone stairs.

It seemed as if Geppetto were trying to get as far away from the mysterious couple as he could.

7.
The Master
Puppeteer

Back in Geppetto's workshop, Pinocchio tried to sit very still. Like a surgeon attending a patient, Geppetto was sanding down a tiny nick the puppet boy had gotten during his fall from the roof. But sitting still was something Pinocchio found very hard to do. He had seen so many new and wonderful things on his first day in the world that he wanted to go back out and play.

Just then there was a knock at the door. Geppetto looked through the window.

"It's Lorenzini, the puppet-show director," Geppetto said with alarm. "And he's got those scoundrels Felinet and Volpe with him. No good can come of this. Those two will do anything for a little money. I saw the way they were looking at you in the street earlier. You would certainly fetch a handsome price if you were for sale. I'll bet they told Lorenzini all about you!"

Geppetto placed Pinocchio on a rack with some other puppet boys. "Stay here and keep quiet,"

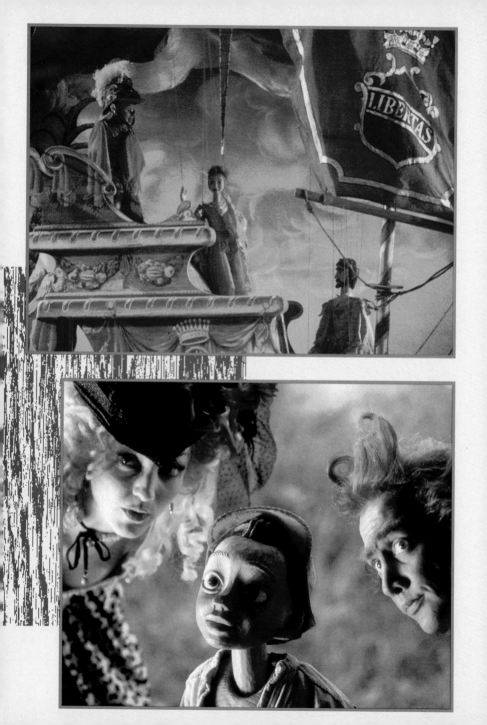

he told Pinocchio. "Don't even breathe. Hear me?"

Pinocchio nodded. He could tell that Geppetto was very upset. He took a deep breath and held it in just as tightly as he could. Then he watched as Geppetto opened the front door and a tall man wearing a long flowing cape stepped inside.

"Geppetto, my friend! Long time, no see," said the man, with a smile that revealed a twenty-four-karat gold tooth. Although the man was smiling, Pinocchio did not think he looked especially friendly.

"To what do I owe the honor of this visit, *Signore* Lorenzini?" Geppetto asked the master puppeteer in a suspicious tone of voice. At the same time, he looked for Felinet and Volpe. But neither of them had entered the house. He finally caught sight of them peeking through the window.

Lorenzini stroked his long black mustache. "The honor is mine," he replied, "to call on the puppet maker with the magical hands. I bring good news, Geppetto. I am mounting my grandest production ever and want to purchase your newest creation. The one I've heard so much about."

Pinocchio saw Geppetto glance back at him. He made sure that he remained as still as he could.

"I don't know what you're talking about," Geppetto said as he politely tried to guide Lorenzini back toward the front door. "But I'll be happy to carve you a little something special the very first chance I get."

Lorenzini scooped up a lamp and sidestepped Geppetto. Acting like a person who knew exactly what he was looking for, he shone the candlelight on a row of puppets. Among them was Pinocchio.

"Lorenzini," Geppetto said, starting to panic. "Those are still being worked on — "

Lorenzini looked carefully at each puppet boy. Pinocchio remained perfectly still, but it was getting harder and harder for him to keep holding his breath. In fact, he was starting to turn blue.

"Hmmm," said Lorenzini. "I was looking for something with, shall we say, thinner strings. . . ."

"Well, why didn't you say so?" Geppetto said, guiding Lorenzini away from the puppet boys. "Over here."

Geppetto led Lorenzini to the other side of the room. There on a shelf were two beautiful puppets. One was a Roman emperor and the other his beautiful daughter.

"Made of the finest cherrywood," said Geppetto as he presented the puppets to the puppeteer. "These sensational works are on sale this week only — "

"Don't toy with me!" Lorenzini snapped back. "I didn't buy these puppets from you two years ago and I'm not buying them today! Now you're aware of the sway I hold in this town. So show me your best, and show me now!"

By now Pinocchio felt as if he were going to explode. Just then a tiny fly began buzzing around his face. It wasn't long before Pinocchio felt the tickle of its wings against his nose. Pinocchio watched the fly until his eyes became crossed. He had never seen such a creature and wanted to play with it. Finally, he could hold his breath no longer. He exhaled. And as he did, the fly went soaring across the room.

Pinocchio leaped off the shelf. "Coming through!" he announced as he chased after the fly and ran right between Lorenzini's legs.

Lorenzini gasped upon seeing the puppet boy with no strings. "He's perfect!" he exclaimed in awe. And with that he caught the fly in the palm of his hand and held it for Pinocchio to see.

Pinocchio was enchanted with the fly.

"Name your price," Lorenzini said, examining the amazing puppet boy closer.

"He's not for sale," said Geppetto.

"Everything's for sale," replied Lorenzini greedily.

"Not him," insisted Geppetto. "Not at any price."

Just then the fly quickly flew out of Lorenzini's palm and out the open window. Just as quickly, Pinocchio chased after it, nimbly climbing to the windowsill and leaning out.

Before he knew it, he went tumbling, head over heels, through the window and into the street.

8.
A School Day

No sooner had Pinocchio landed in the street than he saw a group of boys walking in a single line through the village square.

Pinocchio wondered where the boys were going and decided to fall in line himself. Following at the end of the line for everyone to see made him feel just like a real boy.

In a few moments the boys had reached a schoolhouse, and Pinocchio followed them inside and into a small classroom. There a stern schoolmaster with inch-thick glasses seemed to be waiting for them as they took their seats. Pinocchio did not want to be different from the other boys, so he took a seat just like everyone else.

"Now," said the Schoolmaster. "Resuming our examination of living things, will someone please tell of a characteristic that separates humans from the rest of the animal kingdom?"

"Cages," joked a boy who was seated right next to Pinocchio. Some of the other boys giggled. Pinocchio, again not wanting to be different, giggled, too.

"Lampwick, another remark like that and it'll mean extra homework for you," the Schoolmaster said to the boy who made the joke.

"Humans cry tears, Schoolmaster," another boy offered, raising his hand.

The Schoolmaster smiled. "Ah, yes, tears," he said. "Expressions of the soul. Do any other creatures look so deep into themselves?"

"No, Schoolmaster," replied the same boy. "We must always decide what is right and wrong."

"Excellent!" exclaimed the Schoolmaster happily. Pinocchio could see that he was very pleased.

Just then Lampwick caught sight of Pinocchio. "Hey, Woody," he said. "You ever get termites?"

Pinocchio did not realize that he was the only boy made of wood in the whole class. "What are termites?" he asked.

"Bugs," said another boy.

Pinocchio suddenly remembered the fly he had chased in Geppetto's house. "I like bugs," he said happily.

"Not these kind you don't," said the other boy. "They eat wood like you." Then the boy gave Pinocchio a swift kick in the leg. Since Pinocchio was made all of wood, the kick didn't hurt him at all. In fact, he thought the boy was playing a game with him, so he kicked the boy back just as hard as he could.

"Hey, lay off my friend, Woody," said Lampwick.

"Lay off my friend, Woody," Pinocchio mimicked innocently.

With that Lampwick made a fist and punched Pinocchio. But instead of hurting Pinocchio, Lampwick hurt himself and winced with pain.

Again, Pinocchio thought the boy was playing a fun game with him. So now he made a fist and punched Lampwick right back. Lampwick toppled off his chair and onto the floor.

"What's going on in my class?" the Schoolmaster demanded.

"The new kid punched Lampwick," said one of the boys.

The Schoolmaster threw Pinocchio a stern look. "Is that true?" he asked the puppet boy.

Everybody was now looking at Pinocchio. All at once he knew he had done something wrong, but he wasn't sure what.

"No," he answered, not wishing to tell the truth.

No sooner had he given his answer than Pinocchio's nose started to grow. It didn't stop until it was nearly three feet long.

"Hey, how'd you do that?" asked Lampwick in amazement.

"Silence!" demanded the Schoolmaster. Then he said to Pinocchio, "Now you're not lying to me, by any slim chance, are you?"

"Uh . . . no, Schoolmaster," replied Pinocchio, lying. Then his nose grew another three feet.

"There are two kinds of lies, little one," the Schoolmaster told Pinocchio. "Lies that have short legs and lies that have a long nose. Yours are clearly the kind with the long nose. Now I will give you one more chance to redeem yourself. If you didn't punch Lampwick, how did he end up on the floor?"

Pinocchio didn't know what to do. If he lied, his nose would grow another three feet. But if he told the truth, the whole truth, the other boys in the class might not like him. And he wanted so very much to be liked by everybody else.

"Uh . . . nobody punched Lampwick," he finally replied. "Lampwick punched himself."

And as sure as his answer was a bold-faced lie, his nose grew so long it nearly went clear across the room.

Pinocchio was in a panic. How could he keep his nose from growing? he wondered. Maybe he needed to tell a *different* lie.

"I mean," he began, thinking of something to say, "a man climbed in the window and punched him and Lampwick tried to kick him back but he missed and fell on the floor and — "

By now everyone in the class was howling with laughter, but not just at Pinocchio's story. His nose was growing again. This time it reached so far across the room that it pinned the Schoolmaster against the blackboard and knocked the blackboard eraser right out of his hand.

Clouds of chalk dust from the eraser flew everywhere. It was so dusty that Pinocchio, with his huge nose, began to sneeze.

"Run! Run! Run!" one of the schoolboys shouted as they all ducked for cover.

All, that is, except the Schoolmaster.

"*Ahh — AHH — AHHHHHCHOOOOO!!!*" Pinocchio sneezed and a colossal ball of chalk dust blew right into the Schoolmaster's face. Now the Schoolmaster was covered with chalk.

Pinocchio was trembling in fear, for he knew that what he had done was wrong and that he would certainly be in big trouble now.

"I did punch Lampwick, Schoolmaster," Pinocchio finally admitted. "And I'm sorry."

And with that, Pinocchio's long nose began to shrink.

"Well, it's too late now," said the Schoolmaster. "If there's one thing I will not tolerate in my classroom, it's a liar. Get out!"

Pinocchio tried lowering his head in shame, but his nose, which had not yet returned to its normal size, made that impossible.

"And I'm sorry I kicked him, too," admitted Pinocchio, pointing to the boy he had kicked. With that his nose shrank a few more feet.

"Out, I said," repeated the Schoolmaster.

"And I'm even sorry I told a lie," Pinocchio said,

admitting another truth. This time his nose shrank even further.

"Out! Out, I said!" shouted the Schoolmaster.

"But I want to stay and learn," Pinocchio pleaded.

By now Pinocchio's nose had returned to its normal length. But the Schoolmaster was still pointing to the door for him to leave.

Pinocchio realized he had done a bad thing. He lowered his head in shame and left the room.

9.
Some Sweet Mischief

Pinocchio wandered aimlessly around the village square looking for something to do. He couldn't return to Geppetto's house for fear that Geppetto would ask him where he had been. He knew he couldn't make up a story. That would be a lie. And, as he now knew, every time he lied his nose would grow and grow until he told the truth. In this case, Pinocchio knew, the truth wasn't all that wonderful, either. Geppetto would learn about all the trouble he had gotten into at the schoolhouse. Either way, his papa would be very angry with him.

Just then Pinocchio smelled something fragrant in the air. He found himself standing right in front of a bakery. There were all sorts of freshly baked cakes and cookies and biscuits being laid out for display by the Baker's wife.

Pinocchio suddenly forgot about all his worries. He had begun to feel very hungry, and he went inside the Baker's shop to see about getting something to eat.

The Baker was putting the final touches on a rich, creamy, three-level wedding cake. But when Pinocchio reached his little wooden hand up to snatch a tasty-looking eclair off a table, the Baker saw him right away.

"Don't eat that!" ordered the Baker. But it was too late. Pinocchio's face was covered with chocolate and whipped cream.

Just then the Baker's wife came in carrying a tray full of cookies. When she saw the strange-looking wooden boy stuffing his face with sweets, she shrieked and threw her cookie tray into the air. Pinocchio was showered with falling cookies.

"Mmmm!" he said delightedly. "More!"

"You're a *bad* boy!" said the Baker, pointing his finger at Pinocchio.

"A *real* bad boy," corrected Pinocchio. And with that he began to eat as many cookies, eclairs, and cannoli as he could stuff into his mouth.

"Unhand that cannoli!" demanded the Baker's wife. "It costs 100 *lira*!"

The Baker's wife chased after Pinocchio, who was by now running around the bakery grabbing all the sweets he could find. Soon the entire bakery was covered with half-eaten cupcakes, squashed eclairs, and drooping cakes. Whipped cream and chocolate drops were flying everywhere. Huge bags of flour had split open and were filling the room with powdery white clouds.

The Baker's wife came running at Pinocchio with her baking paddle. She took a swing, but missed, slicing the Baker's freshly made wedding cake in half. The wedding cake teetered and toppled and dropped onto a rickety pile of dishes. The force sent one of the dishes spinning through the air and smashing through the shop window. Broken shards of window glass flew in all directions.

It was at about this time that Pinocchio noticed that a crowd of villagers had gathered at the bakery window. They were trying to see what all the commotion was about. Among them was Geppetto.

"Papa! Are you hungry?" Pinocchio asked, cookies in hand. A look of absolute panic was on the old puppet maker's face.

"Geppetto, he's yours?" asked the Baker's wife. "Then this is all your fault! Arrest him!"

Suddenly a policeman grabbed Geppetto's arm.

"You're under arrest, *signore*," said the policeman.

Pinocchio became very frightened and confused when he saw Geppetto being carted away by a policeman. He dropped all the sweets he was holding and ran to the broken window.

"Papa!" he called. "Papa, why are they taking you away?"

But Geppetto was too far away to hear him.

Pinocchio looked helplessly at the villagers who had crowded around the bakery window, hoping someone would give him an answer. Although no one would tell Pinocchio why the policeman had taken Geppetto away, he could tell from their expressions that it was all because of him.

10.
A New Friend

Pinocchio returned home and warmed himself in front of the fireplace. He was very sad. The Baker's pastry shop had been ruined and Geppetto had been taken away to jail.

And it was all because of him.

"I can't do anything right," he sighed.

"So why don't you jump in?" a high screechy voice came from behind.

Pinocchio spun around, startled at the sound of the voice. But there was no one else in the room.

"Who said that?" Pinocchio demanded, lifting a shoe for protection.

"I must have said it, because there's no one else here," came the screechy voice again. And with that a cricket, no larger than a matchbox, hopped onto a nearby stack of books. "Do you always squoosh someone before being formally introduced?" the cricket asked Pinocchio.

Pinocchio eyed the curious creature with fascination. "Are you a termite?" he asked the bug.

"Oh, puh-lease . . ." the cricket said, insulted.

"So you're not gonna eat me?" asked Pinocchio.

"Why would I eat you?" replied the cricket. "I just had lunch! Allow me to introduce myself. The name is Pugnacio Elocuzio P. Elegante! But you can call me Pepe!"

"Pepe?"

"What," said Pepe. "You don't like it?"

"It's okay." Pinocchio shrugged with indifference.

"Just *okay*?!" demanded Pepe.

"No," said Pinocchio, thinking he had better change his mind so as not to upset this most peculiar creature. "It's fine."

"Now listen up, junior," Pepe the cricket began. "I'm here because you are one mixed-up little puppet. You lied to your teacher, your papa's in jail, you're on the lam. Now I'm much more than just your standard, garden-variety cricket. I'm a teller of truths. Been doin' it a hundred years. Consider me your seeing-eye cricket, pinecone."

"I'm not a pinecone," Pinocchio retorted. "I'm a real boy!"

"Wake up and smell the evergreens," replied Pepe. "You're a puppet! But there's no reason to be ashamed. Some of my best friends owned puppets."

"I don't think I like you," said Pinocchio.

"Hey, that's how the best relationships start out," said Pepe with an encouraging smile. "Six

months from now, we'll be having picnics together. But right now we have to work on your
soul. And all you have to do is everything I say."

Just then there was a knock at the door.

"Get the door," Pepe told Pinocchio. Pinocchio
just stared at the cricket. "I said get the door!"
insisted Pepe. "What do I look like, a butler?"

Pinocchio did as he was told and opened the
door. Several policemen were standing there. Pinocchio smiled. At first he thought they might
have come to bring Geppetto home, but he was
wrong. Geppetto was not with them. Instead, and
much to his surprise, the policemen snatched Pinocchio up and carted him away.

11.
The Trial

"Court is now in session!" said the Magistrate in a deep, booming voice that frightened Pinocchio.

Pinocchio was in a vast courtroom. He was seated all alone in a special dock for the accused. The gallery was filled with spectators. The Baker and the Baker's wife were there. Even Lorenzini the puppeteer was there with Felinet and Volpe.

Then a door at the far end of the room opened and Geppetto, shackled by chains, was escorted in by two policemen.

"Papa!" Pinocchio called out as soon as he saw Geppetto. He ran and wrapped himelf around Geppetto's leg.

"It'll be all right," Geppetto said as he hugged Pinocchio tightly.

Pinocchio could only hope it would be true.

"He did it!" the Baker's wife shouted accusingly, pointing her finger at Pinocchio. "He ruined our cannoli! He ruined our fruit tarts!"

"Silence!" commanded the Magistrate, and he banged his gavel a few times to show that he meant it. Then he faced Geppetto. "Now, since you are reponsible for this . . . puppet," he began. "How do you plead?"

Geppetto paused. "Guilty, sir," he finally admitted with a sigh.

The Magistrate banged his gavel again. "You will pay twenty thousand *lira* to the Baker and ten thousand to the court."

"But that's three years' wages," Geppetto said, stunned.

"If you cannot pay, then you will go to Debtors' Prison. Three years locked away!"

"No!" Pinocchio pleaded as he clung to Geppetto. "Don't go away!"

It was at this moment that Lorenzini swept from the gallery and announced that he had a proposition for the court.

"Your honor," he told the Magistrate. "I propose the court allow me to pay the fines of this poor peasant. All I ask is to keep Pinocchio in return."

"Never!" exclaimed Geppetto.

"Suit yourself," replied Lorenzini. "But who will care for him while you're in prison?"

"Please, Lorenzini," begged Geppetto. "Take any other puppet. I'll work day and night for you for the rest of my life!"

"Tsk, tsk," replied Lorenzini. "Is it just about

money for you? Is gaining employment all you care about?

"Pinocchio needs a home," continued Lorenzini. "All you can offer him are table scraps and cold winter nights. But with me, he'll have . . . a family."

Everyone in the courtroom grew silent.

"What's a family, Papa?" Pinocchio asked Geppetto.

"My goodness," interrupted Lorenzini. "Such a heartbreaking question. One no one should have to ask. Pinocchio, *I* can give you a life other little boys only dream of."

The Magistrate banged his gavel down again and asked Geppetto: "What is your decision, *signore*?"

"Admit it to yourself, Geppetto," Lorenzini added. "In your heart of hearts you know I'm right."

Geppetto remained silent for a long moment. It was easy to see that he was agonizing over his decision. Finally, he bent down and gently said, "Pinocchio, listen to me."

"Yes, Papa?"

"You're going to go with Lorenzini now," said Geppetto.

Pinocchio did not understand. "But I want to be with you," he said.

"I know," said Geppetto, swallowing hard to hold back his tears. "But . . . this is . . . this is the only choice because — "

"You're my papa!" said Pinocchio, confused.

"I can't be your papa," answered Geppetto, unable to look at Pinocchio as he said it. "You're made of wood, not flesh! You're not a real boy. Now go. For everyone's good!" Then Geppetto turned away.

Pinocchio was heartbroken. Why had he been such a mischievous boy, he wondered? If only he had listened to Geppetto in the first place and stayed out of trouble. Then none of this would have happened. He and Geppetto would be able to go home and sit by the nice warm fireplace together like a real father and son.

12.
Opening Night

After the trial, Pinocchio followed Lorenzini to a large theater filled with rows and rows of seats. Some of the rows even reached as high as the rafters. At one end of the theater was a wide stage.

Lorenzini led Pinocchio behind the stage. Here there were many people at work. Some were building things, others were sewing costumes. Everyone was very busy.

Pinocchio had never seen such goings-on and wondered what it was all about.

Finally, Lorenzini brought Pinocchio to a room that was filled with puppets of all shapes and sizes. Some of the puppets, he knew, were the ones Geppetto had made.

"Are you a puppet maker, too?" Pinocchio asked Lorenzini.

"No, little one," Lorenzini laughed. "I am a puppet *master*. These puppets are all actors in my theater. And that is what you are going to be as well. You, my little Pinocchio, are going to be my star attraction."

At first Pinocchio had no idea what Lorenzini meant. He had never been in a theater before, and he certainly didn't know what an actor was. But almost immediately Pinocchio began to learn. Lorenzini explained that Pinocchio was going to be the star of a great entertainment: a stage show with costumes and music. He even said that Pinocchio was going to play the part of the hero.

In a few weeks' time, Pinocchio had learned all his lines and all his music. He had even begun to get excited about performing onstage. He knew that on opening night all the village would turn out to see him, the puppet boy with no strings. Perhaps even Geppetto would come as well.

Pinocchio began to feel like someone special.

Finally, the day of the opening performance arrived. Pinocchio nervously watched from behind the curtains as the theater filled with people. Everybody was there: the Magistrate, the Baker and his wife, Felinet and Volpe, the Schoolmaster. Even some of the kids he had met at school were there.

The only person he did not see was Geppetto.

Pinocchio heard the music from the orchestra swell. Then the curtain rose. The stage was painted to look like a magical, mystical city. On stage a Princess puppet was tied to a stake. Her father, the Roman Emperor, unable to save her, was crying for help.

That was Pinocchio's cue. Sitting on a cardboard cloud, he was lowered down to the stage. As soon as he appeared, the audience cheered wildly.

"Yaaay, Woody!" he could hear Lampwick shout from the audience. Pinocchio felt proud.

Excited, Pinocchio leaped off the cloud to rescue the Princess. But instead of landing on his feet, he tripped and fell headlong into the orchestra pit.

The audience laughed at him.

"Some stringless puppet!" shouted someone from the rafters.

"He can't even stand up!" shouted someone else.

Pinocchio was embarrassed. He stumbled his way through the various musicians in the orchestra pit — stepping on many of their toes as he went — and climbed back onstage.

Pinocchio quickly ran to the Princess and began to untie her, dodging Soldier puppets as he did so. He knew that if he could just concentrate on what he had to do, he wouldn't make any more mistakes. Then everybody would like him.

Suddenly there was a loud roar. A huge Giant puppet was brought onstage to try to stop Pinocchio from rescuing the Princess. Pinocchio jabbed the Giant in the foot with his sword. Everyone in the audience cheered as the Giant howled with pain. Then Pinocchio began running in and out of the Giant's long beard. Try as he might, the Giant couldn't catch Pinocchio. Finally, Pinocchio pinned the Giant's beard to the stage with his sword. The Giant staggered and fell thunderously offstage, defeated by the hero Pinocchio.

Once again the audience cheered. The cheers sent shivers of excitement through Pinocchio. It seemed that everybody liked him now.

Backstage, Pinocchio hugged Lorenzini around the knees. "I love being a star!" he exclaimed happily.

"Of course you do," said Lorenzini. "All real boys love being stars. Stars never die, they shine in their starfire. Like this."

And with that, Lorenzini produced five gold coins as if by magic and poured them into Pinocchio's hands.

"It's all yours, Pinocchio," said Lorenzini.

The light from the coins glittered before Pinocchio's eyes.

"You can buy toys and cakes and anything you want, and after tonight there's much, much more."

Pinocchio still had his arm around Lorenzini when he looked up and saw someone peering down at them from a skylight above. It was Geppetto. The sad look on Geppetto's face pierced Pinocchio's heart like a knife.

When Lorenzini left, Pinocchio found he couldn't take his eyes off Geppetto.

"Not bad, huh?" came the voice of Pepe the cricket. Pinocchio turned around and saw Pepe hanging from a pulley rope. "The applause, the attention, the money. A kid could get used to this. Now all you need is love."

"But I have love," insisted Pinocchio. "Lorenzini loves me."

"The only thing Lorenzini loves is money," said Pepe. "And with you, he knows he can make plenty. Geppetto, on the other hand, doesn't give a cobbler's tack about what you can do for him. All he cares about is what he can do for you. I wonder which one is *real* love?"

Pinocchio paused. He felt confused. "Why do you have to make everything so hard?" he asked the cricket angrily.

And with that he returned to the stage.

13.
A Catastrophe

As Pinocchio returned to the stage, he was greeted by thunderous applause from the audience. He enthusiastically resumed his role as the hero and escorted the Princess onto a great ship. No sooner had the ship gone out to sea than it was attacked by a giant sea monster.

When the sea monster roared, a great flame shot out of its horrifying snout. One of the onstage puppets got caught in the flame and burned to a crisp. With each burst of fire, another puppet went up in flames.

Pinocchio saw that Lorenzini was using a long tube to send fire out of the monster's mouth. Each time another puppet burst into flames, Lorenzini laughed with glee. It seemed to Pinocchio as if Lorenzini was enjoying destroying the puppets!

Next Lorenzini aimed the flame thrower at the Emperor and the Princess. These were two of Geppetto's finest creations. Pinocchio pulled them out of the way.

"Be a smart puppet!" commanded Lorenzini from backstage. "Let them burn!"

"But my papa made them!" replied Pinocchio, as he pulled the Emperor and the Princess out of the way of the flames again. No sooner had he done so than another burst of fire came out of the sea monster's mouth. This time the flames hit the sail of the ship. Now the sail was on fire!

Soon the fire began to spread from the sail to the props and to the painted backdrop. Even the orchestra conductor's baton caught fire.

"Fire!" Pinocchio heard someone shout from the audience. The members of the audience screamed in panic. They began running over one another in an effort to get out of the theater.

Pinocchio bravely carried the Emperor and the Princess puppets away from the flames. Backstage, he found himself face-to-face with Lorenzini. Lorenzini lunged for him, but Pinocchio scooted right between his legs and out the theater door.

Pinocchio was halfway down the outside stairway when suddenly the Emperor's and Princess's puppet strings got caught in the railing. The puppets flew from Pinocchio's grip. Then he himself went tumbling down the stairs headfirst.

Pinocchio quickly got up and dusted himself off. The Emperor and the Princess were lying in a bundle under the stairs. No sooner had Pinocchio moved to gather them up than the theater door shot open and Lorenzini emerged, Felinet and Volpe by his side.

Pinocchio had no choice. He had to leave the puppets and make a run for it. He stepped back into the shadows so he wouldn't be seen. Then he quietly clip-clopped down the dark, lonely cobblestones and away from the smoldering puppet theater.

14.
Looking for Miracles

An hour later, Pinocchio found himself walking through the pine forest at the end of town. He felt good in the forest. He filled his lungs with the fresh smell of pine. The scent seemed to give him renewed strength. He felt safe and sound among the trees because he knew that he was made from them.

"This is where I belong," he muttered to himself.

"I prefer the beach myself," came the voice of Pepe the cricket. "But property there is so expensive."

Pinocchio swiveled around. Pepe was perched on the tip of a fern.

"You can't stay here," Pepe told Pinocchio.

Pinocchio curled himself up into the bark of a fallen tree. "Go away, please," he said as he snuggled to get some rest. "I feel happy here."

"You can't sleep your problems away!" said Pepe. "You've got to get back to your papa!"

" 'Bye . . ." Pinocchio sighed as he began to fall off to sleep.

Just then Pinocchio felt something land on his nose. He half opened one eye and saw that it was Pepe.

"I don't need this, you know," said Pepe. "I have other clients who need help with their souls."

"Then go help Lorenzini," said Pinocchio. And with that he closed his eyes completely.

Now Pinocchio heard a strange tapping noise coming from above. He opened his eyes and saw a woodpecker perched on a branch and looking down at him hungrily. Without warning, the woodpecker leaped off the branch and immediately began pecking on Pinocchio's head.

"Quit it! Ouch!" exclaimed Pinocchio as he tried to fight off the hungry bird. Pinocchio ran away, but the woodpecker followed him, pecking on his head each chance he got.

Pinocchio ran out of the forest and into an old monastery that stood at the side of the road. Slamming the huge monastery door behind him, he was finally safe from the marauding woodpecker.

The monastery was a big, peaceful place. Occasionally monks would pass him. He tried to say something to one of the monks, but the monk raised a finger to his lips. Pinocchio soon learned that a monastery was a place of silence.

Pinocchio came upon a chapel. It was a beautiful room of stone and wood. At the front of the chapel,

Pinocchio saw a plate filled with coins. He remembered that he had such coins in his pocket. They were the ones Lorenzini had given him. He took one of the coins out of his pocket and dropped it into the plate. Then he went to sit down.

A moment later two figures slipped into the seats beside him. They were Felinet and Volpe. Pinocchio recognized them instantly.

"Hey, I know you!" exclaimed Pinocchio in a whisper. "You're friends of Lorenzini."

"But we're finished with him now," said Felinet.

"And we're here to ask for forgiveness," added Volpe.

"What's forgiveness?" asked Pinocchio.

"Forgiveness means that when you do something really wrong, you want somebody to tell you that what you did wasn't *really* really wrong when you know what you did was wrong because you did it."

Pinocchio thought he understood. He lowered his head. "Please forgive me for being a puppet," he said, praying. "Instead of being a real boy for my papa."

"You know," interrupted Felinet. "It *is* possible for you to become a real boy."

"How?" Pinocchio asked eagerly.

"All you need is a miracle."

"What's a miracle?"

"Miracles make your dreams come true," explained Felinet. "In fact, you could buy one with one of those coins you have in your pocket."

"I have four left!" said Pinocchio, excited.

"Unfortunately, you're just a little short," said Felinet. "But you might have enough if — "

"If what?" asked Pinocchio.

"If you planted them and let them grow."

"Where?"

"Why, in the Field of Miracles, of course," said Felinet.

"The Field of Miracles?" asked Pinocchio in awe. "Where is that?"

Felinet and Volpe immediately led Pinocchio to a graveyard behind the monastery. Pinocchio had never seen a graveyard before, so he didn't know what was really buried there. Instead, he believed Felinet and Volpe when they told him that people came there to bury their money and wish for miracles. Then they handed him a shovel and told him to dig a hole.

After a short while Pinocchio had finished digging the hole. When he was done, he placed his remaining coins in the hole just as he had been told. Then he followed Felinet and Volpe to a clock tower.

"Now you stand here and watch that clock," Felinet told Pinocchio. "The big hand will go all the way around and come back to the top. That's one hour. Don't leave a moment sooner, or the gold won't grow."

Pinocchio obeyed Felinet and remained at the clock tower alone. After a moment Pepe drifted by on the nearby stream.

"Outta the woods, huh?" the cricket asked. "What are you doing now?"

"Waiting for an hour to come," replied Pinocchio.

"Why?"

"So I can buy a miracle."

"Who swindled you into that one?" asked Pepe in a suspicious tone of voice.

"Felinet and Volpe," answered Pinocchio. "Here's how it works. You dig a hole, you plant your gold, and let it grow and — "

At that Pepe leaped onto the face of the clock. "Let me ask you this, root rot," he said. "Didn't this gold deal feel a little shaky to you?"

Pinocchio thought for a moment. It was true that he knew that Felinet and Volpe were greedy and clever characters. "I don't know," he told Pepe. "Maybe a little."

"And you went along with it anyway?" asked Pepe.

Pinocchio was silent.

"*Didn't you?*" Pepe asked.

"Maybe," Pinocchio said with embarrassment.

"You don't give 'maybe' to the president of the cricket union," said Pepe. "Look, I like you. Don't ask me why. But you gotta wise up. Now I want you to go back to that hole, get your coins out, take them to your papa, and let him teach you about — "

"My papa wants me to be a real boy," said Pinocchio. "I'm staying right here and waiting for my miracle."

"You know, it's really irritating trying to help someone who insists on thinking for himself," sighed Pepe as he leaped off the clock face. "Go ahead. Wait for a miracle. See if I care. But remember you heard it here first: Miracles don't grow on trees. Miracles are made in the heart."

And with that, Pepe hopped off and disappeared downstream.

When the hour had passed, Pinocchio eagerly set out for the graveyard. He raced back to the spot where he had buried his money, hoping all the while that he would find his miracle once he got there.

But when he arrived, he found someone had dug a hole and taken the money he had planted. There was no miracle at all.

"Stupid me!" shrieked Pinocchio. It wasn't hard for him to figure out that Felinet and Volpe had tricked him.

Pinocchio walked away from the monastery feeling very sad. Finally he got tired of walking and sat down on a rock.

"Miracles don't grow on trees," he kept repeating to himself. "Miracles don't grow on trees."

It was at that moment that a coach, pulled by six ragged donkeys, came teetering down the road. The coach was overflowing with boys of all ages, shapes, and sizes.

"Hey, Woody!" Pinocchio heard one of the boys call to him. It was Saleo, one of the boys he had met at school.

"Come with us," said Lampwick, who was among the boys as well. "We're going to the greatest place! It's brand new. No school and no rules. We can do whatever we want! And it's just for boys!"

Pinocchio jumped up. "Just for boys?"

"Yup," said Lampwick. "Real boys!"

That was all Pinocchio had to hear. So, filled with excitement, he leaped onto the carriage with the other boys. How he longed to go to a place where he would be among real boys. Maybe there he would find the miracle he needed to become a real boy himself. Maybe there he could learn how to become a real son.

15.
Terra Magica

"**Y**AHOO! I'M GOING TO BE A REAL BOY!"
Pinocchio shouted happily as the donkey-drawn coach turned around a bend.

The coach plowed through a gushing waterfall. As it did so, Pinocchio's cap was flushed off his head and carried out to sea.

Pinocchio didn't care about his hat. All he could think about was Terra Magica, the place where he was going with the real boys.

Finally the coach entered a long tunnel hidden behind the waterfall. After moving through the darkness for a few scary minutes, the coach emerged through an opening at the other end of the tunnel.

Pinocchio's eyes grew wide with wonder as he saw Terra Magica for the first time. There was a grand entrance with tall columns. Behind it were lush, green, rolling hills that seemed to extend way into the horizon. Flowers were growing everywhere, even on the trees.

Fireworks exploded in the air, and Pinocchio saw that there were boys everywhere. Some were running, some were playing, some were laughing, some were singing. Some were eating gobs and gobs of cakes and pastries just like the ones Pinocchio had eaten in the Baker's shop.

Suddenly a man in a colorful costume stepped in front of the coach. He was holding a big sign.

"Here are the rules of Terra Magica," said the man. Then he read them off one by one: "No noise. No lying. No playing with fire. Brush your teeth. Respect your elders. Go to bed on time."

The boys frowned with disappointment.

"Hey," said Lampwick. "I thought we were gonna be able to have fun!"

Just then the man smiled and passed out an armful of mallets. "I forgot," he said. "The biggest rule of all is, there are no rules!"

And with that the boys smashed the rule sign to bits with their mallets. No one was happier to do it than Pinocchio.

There were rows and rows of tents in Terra Magica. Pinocchio saw that boys would run into the tents and then come out laughing. It was no wonder, he realized, as he and Lampwick approached one of them. Attendants were standing in front of each tent ready to give out candy to any boy who went inside.

"I hope you like feathers," Lampwick said to Pinocchio, after looking through a window of a tent marked BEDLAM. The boys inside were having a messy pillow fight. "Let's go!"

No sooner had Pinocchio and Lampwick entered the tent than they were bombarded with pillows.

"I hate when my mom makes me go to bed," said a boy as he thwacked Lampwick with a feathery missile of fun.

"I'm staying up forever," said another boy as he whacked Pinocchio silly.

Pinocchio wanted to have some fun, too. So he grabbed a pillow and started swinging back at the boy who had hit him. The boy ducked and Pinocchio went twirling around so fast he became dizzy.

After a while Pinocchio and Lampwick grew tired of fighting with pillows. They left BEDLAM and came upon a very strange place. There were bugs everywhere. There were squiggly ones and squirmy ones and big ones and little ones. Not only that, but some boys were filling ice cream cones with bugs to shoot them in the air!

Pinocchio smiled with joy. After all, he just loved bugs.

Some of the boys were putting bugs at the tips of rockets and blasting them off into the sky. Now it was Pinocchio's turn to do the same. He scooped up a bug in his hand and tied it to a rocket.

"You think I was this thoughtless as a youngster?" Pinocchio heard a familiar voice say. Then he took a closer look at the rocket. The bug he had just tied to it was none other than Pepe, his guardian cricket.

"I'm having fun," replied Pinocchio. "That's what real boys do."

"How would you like it if I started picking off all the puppets in your papa's workshop?" asked Pepe. "And speaking of your papa, since you brought him up — "

"I didn't bring him up," corrected Pinocchio.

"No kidding, tree stump! Now get your fool self back to him. Or do you have a wooden heart as well as a wooden head?"

Suddenly Pepe looked down. Lampwick had just lit the fuse under the rocket.

"I can't go on a trip!" yelled Pepe. "I forgot my toothbrush!" But by then it was too late. The rocket blasted off straight toward the sky.

Pinocchio couldn't remember the last time he had had so much fun.

16.
The Big One

By day's end Pinocchio, Lampwick, and the other boys had been through most of the fun places in Terra Magica. In fact, there was just one more to go. This place was called THE BIG ONE. Here, a huge bin with wheels sat on some tracks. The boys climbed inside and waited to go for a ride.

As soon as they were all safely inside, the bin began to climb ever so slowly up a hill. When it reached the top of the hill, it stopped. Pinocchio peeked out. Behind him he could see all of Terra Magica with its rolling hills and fun places. Before him he could see only a deep, dark tunnel.

Pinocchio wasn't sure why, but for a moment he suddenly felt very frightened. Before he could even wonder why, he felt the chain that held the bin snap. The bin then began to roll down the hill, straight toward the mouth of the tunnel.

The boys screamed with excitement as the bin

rolled downhill. Even Pinocchio was excited. "I'm a real boy," he repeated to himself as if it were a wish come true. "I'm a real boy."

The bin sped through the tunnel at breakneck speed. It passed through a fountain of water.

The boys gulped down the water as they shot through.

Then the bin curved, dipped, and bumped along the tracks. Finally it bounced up in the air and landed again in a burst of sparks.

"Whoa!" said Lampwick as the bin hit the tracks. But this time Lampwick didn't sound like a little boy. He sounded kind of like a donkey.

"What's wrong with your voice?" Pinocchio asked Lampwick.

"I don't feel so hot," said Lampwick. He touched his head to see if he had a fever, but instead he discovered something worse.

He had grown two large donkey ears!

"You look terrible," said Saleo, seeing Lampwick's newly grown ears. "Hey, what's that?" Saleo said, looking down. A donkey tail was sticking out from somewhere. He reached out and grabbed it hard. "Owww!" Lampwick screamed. The donkey tail was sticking out of *him!*

Pinocchio couldn't believe his eyes. In a few short moments his friends had all turned into donkeys, complete with snouts, hooves, and tails!

Then Pinocchio began to feel a little funny. He

reached up and found that his own wooden ears had also grown large. He was beginning to turn into a donkey, too!

Meanwhile the bin raced through a door at the end of the tunnel. Once outside, the bin was immediately wrapped in heavy chains and was brought to a full stop by a huge, mean-looking man with a whip.

"Satisfy your thirst, you donkeys?" asked the man with the whip. "Pretty magical water, eh?"

So it was the water that had changed the boys into donkeys, Pinocchio realized. As he looked all around him, he saw a corral filled with braying, crying boys that had turned into donkeys. And presiding over all of them was Lorenzini, the puppeteer!

17.
Escape from Lorenzini

"**H**ere's another batch, *signore*," the man with the whip told Lorenzini as he presented Pinocchio and the others.

"Get 'em corralled," Lorenzini ordered his foreman.

Pinocchio crouched down in the bin, hoping not to be recognized by the evil puppeteer.

"I don't want to be a donkey," he repeated to himself. "I don't want to be a donkey."

"You should have thought of that before acting like one," came Pepe the cricket's voice. The tiny bug had appeared like magic on a bolt in the side of the bin. "The true self emerges eventually."

"Please, Pepe," Pinocchio pleaded. "Get me out of here!"

"I wish I could," replied Pepe. "But my wings are tied on this one."

"I promise to get back to my papa as soon as I can!"

"Hey," said Pepe. "*You* insisted on being Mr. Big Shot. *You* had to have your own way. And now you're up to your knotholes in — "

But before Pepe could finish his thought, Lorenzini's foreman reached into the bin and grabbed Pinocchio by the ears.

"Hey, here's one we missed!" Lorenzini's foreman called out as he yanked Pinocchio out of the bin.

Upon seeing each other, Pinocchio and Lorenzini let out screams. Just then Lampwick the donkey ran right between them. This gave Pinocchio just enough time to flee.

Pinocchio ran straight for one of the corrals and opened the latch. A horde of donkeys went running in all directions. Suddenly Pinocchio felt someone grab him by the donkey ears. It was Lorenzini.

Pinocchio struggled to escape Lorenzini's grip. It was just then that he saw Lampwick the donkey come racing by. He reached out and grabbed Lampwick by the tail. Now Pinocchio was being pulled in two directions. But when his wooden donkey ears snapped off in Lorenzini's hands, Pinocchio was suddenly free.

He rode Lampwick all the way back toward Terra Magica.

"Get that puppet!" Pinocchio heard Lorenzini order his foreman. "I'm gonna get you, Pinocchio. Do you hear me? I'm gonna get you!"

18.
Lorenzini's Farewell

"**N**O, WAIT!!! DON'T TAKE THAT RIDE!!!" Pinocchio shouted to a bunch of boys as he and Lampwick reached the entrance to THE BIG ONE. "Can't you see what's happening? We've been acting like donkeys, so that's what we turn into!"

The boys stopped as soon as they heard Pinocchio.

A moment later, Lorenzini appeared. He had a big, friendly smile on his face.

"Now, now, Pinocchio," he said. "A good boy doesn't go around telling lies."

Pinocchio could tell that Lorenzini would say anything to persuade the boys to take the ride and become donkeys.

"It's not a lie!" Pinocchio told the boys. "My nose grows when I lie!"

"Get in, kids," Lorenzini told everybody. "The ride is fun!"

"No!" shouted Pinocchio. "Don't!" And with

that Pinocchio nudged Lampwick's side with his heels. Lampwick whinnied and brayed and kicked Lorenzini into the gushing water at the entrance of the big ride. It was the very same water that turned Pinocchio's friends into donkeys.

Lorenzini thrashed about in the water, trying to get out from under it. But try as he might, he still swallowed quite a bit of it, and soon he, too, began to change. Red veins began to bulge out of his eyes and temples, his head began to grow and grow, and his ears began to disappear. Soon his body had grown so large that his clothes began to pop off. Lorenzini was turning into some kind of monster, which was just how he had been behaving all along.

He ran as far away from everybody as he could, stumbling blindly as he went. Before long he had reached some cliffs. Pinocchio could see that if Lorenzini didn't stop soon, he would fall off the cliffs into the sea far below.

Which is exactly what he did.

They all cheered when Lorenzini fell off the cliff.

"Let's get out of here!" the boys said. Now all the boys and donkeys began to run away.

Pinocchio headed down a road, looking for a way out. Lampwick clip-clopped along by his side. When they were far enough away from Terra Magica, Pinocchio said, "I don't care anymore if I never become a real boy. I just want to go home to my papa."

"There you are!" Pinocchio heard someone say. He looked up and saw Leona. She was walking down a hill toward him. Pinocchio ran into her waiting arms and hugged her as if she were his mama.

"Where have you been? You look so skinny!" Leona asked as she hugged him.

"Where's my papa?" was all Pinocchio could ask.

Leona pointed out to sea. "I wish I knew. He's out there somewhere looking for you. When he found your cap washed up on shore, your papa thought you had drifted out to sea. He took a boat and went to find you."

Without hesitating for a single moment, Pinocchio began running toward the sea.

"Wait, Pinocchio!" Leona called out after him. "It's too dangerous!"

But Pinocchio didn't stop. Instead, he jumped into a small boat and set out to find his papa.

Pinocchio spent the next several hours at sea, in the small rowboat. He searched high and low for Geppetto.

"Papa!" he would call out. "Papa!" But no matter how fast he rowed or how far he went, he couldn't find Geppetto.

By late in the day, the sun had started to go down. The waters of the ocean were still and calm. Pinocchio was beginning to give up all hope of finding Geppetto.

Suddenly he felt a wave rise beneath his boat and carry him farther out to sea. The wave was so big that it lifted Pinocchio's boat several feet into the air. Pinocchio had never felt a wave this big before, and he looked down to see what had caused it.

To Pinocchio's surprise, it wasn't a wave at all. It was a big, bulgy-eyed, green-scaled sea monster. And it looked exactly like Lorenzini!

Without warning, the sea monster opened its huge jaws. Inside was a big green tongue. And it was surrounded by a hundred jagged teeth. One of the teeth was solid twenty-four-karat gold.

It *was* Lorenzini, Pinocchio realized! He had been transformed into a sea monster by the magic water back at Terra Magica.

"I'm not scared," Pinocchio told himself, shaking.

No sooner had he said that than the sea monster swallowed him whole, boat and all, and clamped its giant jaws tight.

19.
Inside a
Sea Monster

It was dark inside the sea monster. It was so dark that Pinocchio could not even see his own fingers. But it wasn't long before Pinocchio's eyes began to adjust to the darkness. Soon he was able to make out a few shadowy shapes. The inside of the sea monster was as deep and as high as a cavern. Seaweed and fish skeletons were everywhere. Rubbish littered the beast's insides. This sea monster seemed to swallow everything that crossed its path.

Pinocchio shook some seaweed from his head and pulled off an oyster that had somehow gotten attached to his nose. He was about to toss the oyster away when he heard a knocking sound coming from the shell. Someone was inside the oyster! He pried it open as quickly as he could.

"Ahoy, captain!" came a familiar voice from the oyster. It was Pepe.

Pinocchio was so happy to see his little friend. "Pepe!" he exclaimed. "I thought you left me!"

"Where are we?" asked Pepe, looking around. "I'm sensing the malodorous waftings of rotten chili peppers."

"We're inside Lorenzini," explained Pinocchio. "He became a sea monster."

Even Pepe was scared by the thought. "Nice to know ya," he said, starting out of the oyster. "I'm playing cricket this afternoon."

Pinocchio quickly shut the oyster shell. Pepe was trapped inside.

"I'm afraid of the dark!" shouted Pepe.

"Quiet," said Pinocchio. "We're in this together."

And with that Pinocchio put the oyster in his pocket and began to make his way deeper into the belly of the sea monster.

"Papa?" Pinocchio called out as he walked. "Papa?"

"Oh, sure," he heard Pepe say from inside his pocket. "Like he's just around the corner."

"He might be," Pinocchio said in a hopeful tone of voice.

Pinocchio ignored the little cricket and kept searching. "Papa?" he repeated. "Papa?"

"Pinocchio?" came a weak voice from the shadows. "Oh, if only it were true. . . ."

Pinocchio recognized the voice instantly. It was Geppetto.

"Papa!" Pinocchio called out and raced forward. Sure enough, there, sitting atop a mound of garbage in a gooey pool was Geppetto.

"Papa!!!" exclaimed Pinocchio happily as he hugged Geppetto.

"Pinocchio!" said Geppetto. His eyes were filled with tears. "Where have you been?"

"Oh, Papa, I've missed you so," said Pinocchio.

"I've missed you, too," replied the puppet maker. "Come on. Let's try to get out of here! This way. That looks like the throat up ahead."

Pinocchio climbed on Geppetto's back. Then the two of them made their way through the cavernous belly of the sea monster, wading through water and slimy goo as they went.

When they finally reached the opening of the sea monster's throat, they saw that it was very narrow. In fact, it was only big enough for Pinocchio to get through, not Geppetto.

"Go," Geppetto told Pinocchio.

"Not without you," said Pinocchio.

"Go, I said!" ordered Geppetto a second time.

"No!" replied Pinocchio. "Push it open!"

But try as he might, Geppetto was unable to stretch the passageway.

Then Pinocchio got an idea. "I hate you, Papa," he told Geppetto.

Geppetto seemed stunned and confused by Pinocchio's words. "What?"

"I never, ever missed you!" insisted Pinocchio.

"That's a lie!" said Geppetto.

And sure enough, it was. And because he had

lied, Pinocchio's nose began to grow and grow and grow.

"And I wish I never found you," Pinocchio added, so his nose would grow even longer. "I never wanted to be your son! I wanted to stay a puppet!"

By now Pinocchio's nose had grown several feet long. He was very happy. His nose was now long enough for him to push it deep into the narrow opening of the sea monster's throat. No sooner had he done this than the sea monster's throat began to expand. Soon its throat was so wide that Geppetto was able to start to crawl through.

But then, *SNAP!* Pinocchio's nose broke under the strain. A small piece broke off and lodged itself in the sea monster's throat. The sea monster began to gag and cough, sending Geppetto and Pinocchio tumbling each time it did so.

Finally the sea monster let out one cough that was so big, it hurled Pinocchio and Geppetto forward and out of its mouth as if they were being shot out of a cannon. The two soared high into the sky before hurtling downward into the sea.

20.
The Real Boy

The sea engulfed Pinocchio and Geppetto. Pinocchio managed to swim safely to the surface, but when he looked around he saw that Geppetto was floating unconscious on the water.

Pinocchio raced toward Geppetto. Then he placed his arms around the old puppet maker and guided him carefully through the sea and to the shore.

"Are you okay, Papa?" Pinocchio asked, as soon as they were safely out of the water. "Wake up!"

After a moment, Geppetto slowly opened his eyes. He reached out and touched Pinocchio.

"Forgive me, Pinocchio," he said weakly. "For doubting my heart and letting you go."

"I'm sorry, too, Papa," said Pinocchio. "I'm sorry for not being a real boy."

Geppetto took Pinocchio in his arms. "You're real to me, my son," he told his puppet boy. "Real to me. Oh, I love you."

Pinocchio felt his heart swell. "I love you, too, Papa," he said.

Just then Pinocchio felt something rise up from his heart, through his throat, and right out of his eyes. It was a teardrop. The teardrop fell, rolling down his cheek and off his face until it landed on the heart that was carved on his little wooden chest.

As if by magic, the teardrop-dampened heart began to pulsate and grow. Then it began to beat like a real heart. All of a sudden Pinocchio began to feel different. Real flesh pushed out from beneath his wooden arms and legs. Real fingers thrust through his wooden ones. His wooden eyes gave way to soft, moist ones. His painted hair became soft and fine, like a real boy's.

Finally Pinocchio's splintered wooden nose fell away and a shiny, round real one took its place.

Pinocchio had become a real boy.

"Tell me it's true!" exclaimed Geppetto with happiness.

Pinocchio knew it was true. And he knew why, too. "Miracles are made in the heart, Papa," he said, remembering something Pepe the cricket had once told him.

Just then Pinocchio heard a tapping sound coming from inside his pocket. It was Pepe, who was still trapped inside the oyster. Pinocchio took the oyster out of his pocket and opened it.

"I don't even want to know what happened,"

said Pepe as he leaped up. He now had his suitcase with him. "Well, nice to know ya, junior. Lotsa luck. See ya. Bye-bye, baby. Gotta go. Yours truly is outta here."

"You're leaving me again?" asked Pinocchio. "I'm just starting to have a good time!"

"No, no," replied Pepe. "I wish I *could* leave. Union rules: I'm stuck with you. You're a lifetime assignment. I just gotta get some sleep!"

And with that Pepe reached up and closed the oyster shell.

By now Geppetto had risen to his feet, fully recovered. "Let's go home," he said, taking Pinocchio by the hand.

No sooner had they started off than they saw Leona approaching them.

"Look at you," Leona told Geppetto. "You're a mess."

"You spend a whole night inside a whale," replied Geppetto. "Let's see how good you look."

"You're sandy and salty and slimy," observed Leona.

"Ah, but I'm alive," said Geppetto.

Leona looked at Pinocchio and smiled. "And so is your son," she said.

And with that, the three of them headed down the shore and back toward the village. Leona had her Geppetto. Geppetto had his real son. And Pinocchio had his miracle.